213 VALENTINES

Chapter books from Henry Holt and Company:

Boo's Dinosaur
Betsy Byars, illustrated by Erik Brooks

Dragon Tooth Trouble
written and illustrated by Sarah Wilson

Fat Bat and Swoop
written and illustrated by Leo Landry

Lavender
Karen Hesse, illustrated by Andrew Glass

Little Horse
Betsy Byars, illustrated by David McPhail

Little Horse on His Own
Betsy Byars, illustrated by David McPhail

Little Raccoon
Lilian Moore, illustrated by Doug Cushman

Sable
Karen Hesse, illustrated by Marcia Sewall

Sea Surprise
written and illustrated by Leo Landry

The Secret Lunch Special (Second-Grade Friends, Book I)
Peter Catalanotto and Pamela Schembri,
illustrated by Peter Catalanotto

213 VALENTINES

Barbara Cohen

Illustrated by
Wil Clay

HENRY HOLT AND COMPANY • NEW YORK

for Levi and Jacob

Henry Holt and Company, LLC
Publishers since 1866
175 Fifth Avenue
New York, New York 10010
www.HenryHoltKids.com

Henry Holt® is a registered
trademark of Henry Holt and Company, LLC.

Library of Congress Cataloging-in-Publication Data
Cohen, Barbara.
213 valentines / Barbara Cohen; illustrated by Wil Clay.
Summary: Wade has trouble adjusting when he is transferred
to a special fourth-grade class for the gifted and talented,
so he plans to send himself 213 valentines signed by celebrities.
[1. Schools—Fiction. 2. Gifted children—Fiction.
3. Valentine's Day—Fiction. 4. Afro-Americans—Fiction.]
I. Clay, Wil, ill. II. Title. III. Title: Two hundred thirteen valentines.
PZ7.C6595Aaf 1991 [E]—dc20 91-7151

ISBN-13: 978-0-8050-2627-6 / ISBN-10: 0-8050-2627-4
Published in hardcover in 1991 by Henry Holt and Company
First paperback edition—1993
Printed in Mexico

20 19 18 17 16 15 14 13

Contents

213 VALENTINES

Gifted and Talented

O kay," Mr. Peretti said. "I want each of you to put your name on a little piece of paper. Marcus, can I borrow your Cubs cap?"

"What for?" Marcus asked.

"You'll all put your names in the cap. Then everyone will pick a name. You have to send a valentine to the person whose name you pick."

Wade groaned. "Valentines? You mean we have to celebrate Valentine's Day?"

"We always celebrate Valentine's Day," Mr. Peretti said.

"Not at Roosevelt School we didn't," Wade said.

"Is that true, Dink?" Mr. Peretti asked.

"The girls sent valentines," Dink replied. "Mostly the boys didn't."

"At Kennedy School, *everyone* sends valentines," Mr. Peretti said.

Then what am I doing here? Wade wondered for about the nine thousandth time. He remembered picking up the mail one day last April and seeing a letter addressed to his uncle from the office of the superintendent of schools. He wasn't concerned. In the third grade at Roosevelt School, he was in the highest reading group, the highest math group, the highest everything. He had nothing to worry about from the superintendent. But had he known that letter was going to ruin his life, he'd have flushed it down the toilet instead of handing it over to Uncle along with the gas bill and the newspaper.

Uncle read the letter out loud: " 'In every way your nephew, Wade Thompson, is a superior student. In mathematics his performance is at a near-genius level. . . .' "

"I ain't no genius," Wade interrupted.

Uncle went right on reading. " 'Therefore he has been chosen as one of the twenty-five pupils in the district to attend the fourth-grade class for gifted and talented students at Kennedy School, starting in September.' "

"I ain't going," Wade said. "I ain't leaving the guys."

"What do you mean, you Ain't going?" Uncle said. "You can bet your Behind you're going. This is a Great Opportunity." Uncle was a conductor for Amtrak trains. One of his jobs was to announce the stations. Wade figured that was why a lot of his words came out sounding capitalized, even in the middle of a sentence.

Wade turned to Auntie Mae. "Do I have to?"

"Uncle is right," Auntie Mae replied softly. "This is a great opportunity. And your friends will still be here, when you get home from school."

"Which is One Thing *I'm* sorry about," Uncle snapped.

"Wade has some very nice friends," said Auntie Mae. "They like to have a good time is all. I remember someone else who liked a good time once."

Wade guessed she must have meant Uncle, because Uncle didn't say another word about Wade's friends.

After supper Wade called his mother. When his parents divorced, his mother had needed a better job. She was staying with her cousin in Milwaukee while she learned fancy computer stuff. "Ma," Wade said, "please tell Uncle I don't have to go to any dumb old gifted and talented class."

"You live with Uncle, you do what Uncle says."

"But Ma . . ."

"It's a great opportunity. I'm proud of you. What do you want for your birthday?"

"Fourth grade at Roosevelt School."

His mother laughed. "No, Wade, what do you want, really?"

"That's what I want, really."

"I'll send you some summer clothes, and twenty-five dollars so you can pick out something yourself. Put Auntie Mae on now. I want to talk to her."

Wade handed the phone to his aunt and left the second-floor apartment in the four-family house where he lived. He ran down the stairs and down the street to Woodlawn Park, where he knew his friends would be hanging out. Woodlawn Park was an odd name for a place in which Wade had never seen either a tree or a blade of grass. It did contain a basketball court, though, and his men were there, watching the big guys play.

"Hey, Junior," Wade said, "did your father get a letter today from the superintendent of schools?" Junior was in the highest everything too.

"Jeez, no," Junior replied. "Why would the superintendent write to my father?"

If Junior hadn't gotten a letter, then the others

certainly hadn't. But Wade asked anyway, just in case. "What about you, Carlos?"

"I don't think so."

"Big Bert?"

"Nah."

"Ali?"

" 'Course not."

"Scott?"

"How would I know?"

"Honch?"

"What's this all about?"

Wade sat down on the low stone wall. "I got chosen for G&T at Kennedy School. Uncle says I have to go."

"That's a drag," Junior said. "I'd quit school if they made me go all the way across town."

"Listen, dumbo," Honch said, "you can't quit in the fourth grade."

"I don't want to quit," Wade said. "I just want to stay at Roosevelt. Nothing but rich nerdy snobs at Kennedy School. All the kids from Woodlawn Park go to Roosevelt." Their treeless neighborhood carried the same name as their treeless park.

"I got an idea," Ali said. "Just act dumb. You know, like you can't read, you can't multiply. . . ."

"That's right, Wade," Scott said, "act just like Ali."

"Shut your big mouth," Ali retorted, "or I'll deck you."

"Cut it out, guys," Wade cried. "This is serious."

But no one came up with a better idea than Ali's. And Wade knew Ali's idea wouldn't work. It was too late for that.

The school year wound down. Nothing more was said about the gifted and talented class. After a while Wade stopped worrying about it. Then summer came, and he was much too busy hanging out with the guys to think about school. They played basketball when the big guys would let them near the court. They rode buses to the municipal pool and went swimming. The seven of them ran in a screaming line down the street, driving pedestrians crazy. Unfortunately, Uncle caught that act and made Wade stay in the apartment four hot nights in a row. One Sunday Auntie Mae took them for a picnic in Haliburton Park, which besides trees and grass actually had flowers and a lake. She brought along enough fried chicken, biscuits, angel food cake, and Coca-Cola to feed the United States Marines. Between one thing and another, Wade nearly forgot there was such a thing as school.

September came as a nasty surprise. One hazy, damp morning he found himself climbing into a van to be driven to Kennedy School. It arrived at Wood-lawn Park so early none of the guys were out on the street yet. Wade was glad of that. At least he didn't actually have to say good-bye to anyone.

The van held only one other passenger. Wade knew her name, because in third grade she, too, had been in the highest everything. But he'd never paid any attention to her.

"Hello, Wade," she said shyly.

"Hi, Dink," he replied. She was sitting in the middle, so Wade climbed into the back.

"I didn't know you were going to G&T too."

"I wish I weren't," he replied grimly. "No one else from Woodlawn Park will be there."

"I don't mind."

"That's because you're not leaving any real good friends."

"I am too," she protested. "Elaine and Keesha, aren't they my good friends? But I can still play with them after school. I don't have to stay at Roosevelt for that."

She, too, seemed to think the gifted and talented class was a great opportunity. He couldn't imagine that she still thought so by the time the first morning was over. The other kids in G&T lived in the Foothills.

They arrived in groups of five and six from Eisenhower, Taft, and Lincoln schools. The way they came shouting and giggling into the classroom, you'd think they were hitting Disneyland instead of fourth grade. When Mr. Peretti finally got them to shut up, he assigned them seats alphabetically. "That's so you'll get to know kids from other schools," he explained. "We're here to make new friends, not just hang out with old ones." Then he made everyone announce their names and what schools they'd come from.

The kids clapped when they heard a friend announce the name of their former school—all except Wade Thompson and Dink Worth. One person clapping doesn't sound like much.

Thompson came before Worth. "Wade Thompson," Wade said. "Roosevelt School."

"Roosevelt School!" Allison Keller exclaimed. "I never knew anyone from Roosevelt School before. Do you live in Woodlawn Park?"

"What of it?" Wade snapped.

"I never knew anyone who lived in Woodlawn Park before," Allison continued. "Are you sure you're in the right room?"

"You'd better believe he's in the right room," Mr. Peretti announced. He looked down at the seating chart in his hand. "All right, Evelyn, you're next." Evelyn Torrance was black too, but she'd been at Kennedy School all along.

Dink's turn came soon after. "Darlene Worth," she said. "Roosevelt School. My little niece can't say Darlene, so she calls me Dink. Everyone else does too."

"Dinka-dinka-dink," Allison sang. "Is Wade your boyfriend?"

"Of course not," Dink returned instantly.

"That's enough, Allison," Mr. Peretti said. "If you have anything else to say, raise your hand and wait to be called on. I'm warning you, it'll probably be a long wait."

"She was just teasing," Farley McNair said. Mr. Peretti ignored him.

After the introductions, Mr. Peretti made a homework assignment. "Write a composition about your summer vacation," he said.

Wade had thought that at least G&T might be good for an original composition topic. Back at Roosevelt, he'd have made a smart crack about having to write on the same subject every fall. Here at Kennedy, he thought he'd better keep his mouth shut.

"Shall we write the composition on our computers?" Allison asked.

"That'll be good," Mr. Peretti replied.

"Some people might not have computers," Marcus Silverman said. He sat next to Dink.

"Of course I meant to do it on your computer if you have a computer, and want to use it," Mr. Peretti explained. "Otherwise, just write it in ink."

The next day Mr. Peretti made them read their compositions out loud. Allison had spent two weeks on a Greek island. Marcus had gone to hockey camp. Farley had gone with him. Ellie Nakamura had flown out to her grandparents' pineapple farm in Hawaii. Dink had played Barbie dolls with Keesha and baby-sat her niece. Wade wished he'd written that he'd gone to the moon instead of the municipal pool.

"I gave it two days," Wade told Uncle that night. "I'm not going back tomorrow. Those kids are all stuck-up snobs."

"There's not another black kid in the class?" Auntie Mae asked. "That's not good. I can't believe you're the only smart black kid in the district."

"There's a whole lot of Smart Black Kids in the District," Uncle said. "The Question is, does the District know it?" He turned to Wade. "Well?"

"Well what?"

"Are there any other black Kids in your class?"

"Dink Worth," Wade admitted, "and two others. But they're from the Foothills. One went to Taft School, and the other's been at Kennedy all along."

"So they're in the same boat as you," Auntie Mae said. "They don't know anyone either."

"Yes, they do. There're six other kids from Taft, and three from Kennedy."

"Well, you've got Dink," Auntie Mae suggested.

"Dink!" Wade exclaimed. "She's not only a girl, she's a nerd. There's nothing worse than a lady nerd. And I had to eat lunch with her two days in a row, because there wasn't anyone else to eat with. At Roosevelt School I never even said hello to her."

"That wasn't so nice," Auntie Mae commented quietly.

Uncle was swelling up like a bullfrog. "No one asked you to Eat with him? No one?"

Wade was afraid Uncle would explode. "Marcus Silverman did. I told him no thanks."

"Why?"

"You know what Marcus said? When Mr. Peretti told us to write our compositions on our computers he said, 'Maybe some kids don't have computers.' He was talking about me and Dink."

"He could have been trying to tell the teacher something," Auntie Mae remarked, "something the teacher needed to know."

"No way. He was putting us down."

"I'll get you a Computer," Uncle said.

"I'd rather have a dirt bike," Wade replied. "But mostly, I'd rather be back at Roosevelt School."

"You're going to Give Up, just like that?" Uncle boomed. "You're going to let them Beat you Down? Nothing doing. You're staying in that class. You got No Choice."

2

A Box as Big as a Skyscraper

Toward the end of October, Mr. Peretti asked Wade to stay behind at lunchtime. He sat down at the desk next to Wade's, even though he'd have been much more comfortable if he'd called Wade up to his own desk. The knees of his long legs almost touched his chest. "You going to wear a costume for the Halloween party?" he asked.

Wade shook his head. "Costumes are dumb."

"We always wear costumes for Halloween at Kennedy School."

"I'm not at Kennedy School because I want to be at Kennedy School," Wade said. "I want to be at Roosevelt School."

"Still?" Mr. Peretti asked. "In spite of the Math Club?"

"That's the only reason I stay." The Math Club and Uncle, Wade added to himself.

"So it isn't all bad around here, is it?"

"I never said it was," Wade returned. "But I'm not wearing a dumb Halloween costume." And he didn't.

The Math Club *was* good. Wade liked the competitions with other schools. Mostly Kennedy School won, and he was one big reason why. It was almost like being on a basketball team, though he hadn't said a word about the Math Club to the Woodlawn Park gang. He didn't think it would seem like a basketball team to them.

For Christmas, he got a computer. "Thank you, Uncle," he said. "Thank you, Auntie Mae." He knew it hadn't been an easy thing for them to buy. But he still wished the computer were a dirt bike. Junior got a dirt bike. He let the guys take turns zooming across the gravel paths in the park. That gave Wade an idea. "You want to come up and fool around with my computer?" he asked. Scott and Junior took him up on his offer once or twice, but then they went on to other things.

By February there wasn't much about that computer Wade didn't know. He wrote letters on it to his mother. Besides going to school, she had a part-time job, and she answered him on the word processor she used at work. He wrote compositions for school on his computer too. He took programming books out of the school library and taught himself Basic. He invented and then solved all kinds of math problems. Still, he wanted a dirt bike.

In addition to the Math Club, he now belonged to the Computer Club. So there were two good things about Kennedy School. Sending valentines was one of the twenty-seven bad things.

As he picked a name out of the cap, Wade glanced at Dink and shook his head. Dink looked at Wade and shrugged. He figured she'd get just one valentine, from whoever picked her name. He might actually get two, one from whoever picked his name and one from Dink. Unless of course, Dink picked his name. Then it was back to just one. Allison would get fifty-two, at least. Marcus would get thirty-eight. Actually, everyone in the room except him and Dink would probably receive piles of valentines.

"Hey, Dink," he asked at lunch, "whose name did you pick?"

"Farley McNair."

"That snob."

"Yeah," she agreed. "I'm not going to spend more than ten cents on his valentine. He got my name at Christmas. He gave me a comic book. I think it was used."

"You can't even get a valentine for ten cents," Wade said, "except from one of those punch-out books. And there's no point in buying a book, because who would you send the other ones to?"

"Maybe I'll send one to Angie DiCarlo. What name did you pick?" Dink asked.

"Ellie Nakamura. She's a snob too. They're all snobs."

Slowly Dink shook her head. "They're not *all* snobs."

"They're not?"

"Angie is all right. She chose me for her dodgeball team. She always chooses me for her team."

"They're all snobs," Wade repeated.

Dink said nothing.

"They are," Wade insisted. "If they weren't, you'd be eating lunch with some of them."

Dink chewed hard and swallowed. When she spoke, Wade could hardly hear her. "Angie asked me to eat with her."

"What?"

"I said Angie asked me to eat with her."

"So why didn't you?"

This time, Dink made no reply.

And then, suddenly, Wade knew why Dink hadn't gone with Angie. She didn't want to leave him eating lunch alone! She didn't know that Marcus had invited him to sit at his table. This skinny, snot-nosed little girl was protecting him! It was hard for Wade to believe he'd sunk so low. He finished his bologna sandwich and chocolate milk in silence. He had a lot to think about.

The day after they'd picked the names out of the Cubs cap, Mrs. Krause, the art teacher, showed up lugging a cardboard box so big a refrigerator must have come in it. "We're going to decorate this box for your valentine mail," she said.

The other kids cut paper hearts out of red construction paper. Wade worked on problems in his math book. Mrs. Krause walked over to his desk. "Wade, this is your valentine box too," she said.

"I have all this math to get done," he said.

She glanced at the page he was working on. It was page 379. "But Wade, you're at the end of the book," she said. "That's for June."

"If I finish, Mr. Peretti will give me the fifth-grade book."

"I think it would be good for you to take a little time out to have some fun," Mrs. Krause suggested.

"Math is fun," Wade said. "For me." He glanced at her from beneath his thick, black lashes. "In G&T teachers are supposed to encourage your natural abilities."

Mrs. Krause raised her eyebrows. But for the rest of the hour, she left him alone.

A warm spell had melted the snows of January, and then the temperature had dropped again. After school Wade, Scott, and Junior skateboarded across the blacktop in the park. They had the whole place to themselves. It was too cold for most kids to hang around outside. Darkness fell early, and Wade went in to start his homework. Uncle and Auntie Mae both got home about six, Uncle from the railroad and Auntie Mae from Lamont Memorial Medical Center where she worked in admissions. After dinner Wade finished his homework, watched a little TV, talked to Junior on the telephone, and went to bed.

In bed, he read for a while. It was a book Mr. Peretti had given him about the Civil War, and it was pretty interesting. He had to finish it in a week so he could write a book report about it. When he shut out his light, he thought his mind would be full of the smoking guns and blood-stained corpses of the Battle of Gettysburg. But instead all he saw was an enormous box covered in white lace doilies and red hearts. He opened his eyes wide. He stared at the shadows on the ceiling cast by the light of the street lamp coming through the slatted blind on his bedroom window. Then he shut his eyes. There was that box again, big as a skyscraper. Only this time it was transparent. He could see that it was full of valentines. He could even read the names on them. In that whole box there wasn't one valentine addressed to him.

He sat up in bed and turned on the lamp. "I don't care," he said to himself. "I know I'll get one valentine, maybe two. And I don't care if I don't get any." He shut the lamp and lay down, staring again at his striped ceiling. There, in the silence and the darkness, he admitted to himself that he did care.

In the van on Monday morning he talked to Dink. "I'll get those snobs. I'll get those rich, snooty creeps."

"You can't fight ten guys all by yourself," Dink said.

"Oh, Dink, use your head. I'm not going to fight them. I'm going to show them."

"What are you going to show them?"

"I'm just going to show them. I'm going to get more valentines than anyone else in the class. I'm going to get so many valentines that humongous box won't hold them all."

"How?" Dink wondered.

"Jeez, Dink, for a smart girl you can really be dumb. Can't you figure it out?"

She thought for a moment. "You're going to send them to yourself."

"That's right."

"But if I could figure that out, won't everyone else be able to figure it out too?"

"I'm going to sign each one different."

"Oh."

"I'll buy them this afternoon." He didn't feel like going to the store by himself. But he didn't want Junior and Scott and the rest of the guys to know what he was doing. They thought at Kennedy School he was the same big wheel he'd been at Roosevelt School. Only Dink knew that in G&T he counted for less than zero, and she would never tell. "You want to meet me at K Mart?"

"Sure," she said, with a grin so enormous he thought her face was going to split in half. She didn't

offer to walk over with him after school. She knew he
wouldn't want to be seen on the street with her.

When the van dropped him home, he ran up to the
apartment, opened the door carefully, slipped inside,
and bolted it behind him. In his bedroom, he closed
the blind, knelt down in front of the closet, and
reached into the farthest, darkest corner. There, behind old shoes, he felt the metal box once filled with
Danish butter cookies someone at the hospital had
given Auntie Mae for Christmas. He pulled it out of
the closet, opened it, and sat on the floor counting his
money. He hadn't spent a penny that his mother sent
him on special occasions in nearly a year. He was
saving up for a dirt bike. But this was an emergency.

He counted his stash. He had one hundred and ten
dollars. Mr. Peretti had taught them about interest.
He supposed he ought to open up a savings account
in a bank so his money would make money. It would
be safer there, too. Well, he'd do that the next time
his mother sent him some.

He took twenty-five dollars from the box, closed it
up, and stuffed it back in the corner of his closet. He
rolled the bills up and shoved them in his pocket.
Then he left the building and walked three blocks to

K Mart. He was glad he didn't run into anyone he knew.

Dink was waiting for him in the card department. He took the money out of his pocket and showed it to her. "I've been saving up for a dirt bike. So I'll just have to save a little longer. This is more important."

Dink looked doubtful.

"Well, it is," he added defensively. "Right now, it is."

He picked up eight punch-out valentine books from the counter. "You're going too fast," Dink said. "Look them over, make sure they're the ones you really want."

"What difference does it make?" he returned. "They're all the same, a lot of red hearts and dumb sayings." There were twenty-five valentines in each book, with envelopes. That made two hundred valentines, and they cost a fortune, twenty-four dollars. The tax came to a dollar forty-four. "I'm forty-four cents short," he said.

"I'll lend it to you," Dink said. She pulled a ten-dollar bill out of her purse.

"Where'd you get that kind of money?" Wade wondered.

"Sometimes my sister pays me for baby-sitting."

"Do you think you could lend me a little more? I'd like to buy some big valentines too. I don't want them all to look the same. Thirteen big valentines at fifty cents each. That would be six dollars and fifty cents plus thirty-nine cents tax, seven thirty-three altogether." Numbers danced together in Wade's head like a music video. "Don't worry, I'll pay you back soon as I get home."

"Oh, I'm not worried," Dink said. "If I give you seven thirty-three, it'll still leave me enough to buy five valentines. That's all I need, five valentines. I'll just spend a quarter on Farley's, and then I can spend fifty cents on one for my mother and one for my niece and one for Angie."

"That's only four."

She shrugged and turned away. "Never you mind about that."

Wade didn't want Dink wasting her precious money on a valentine for him. "Do you think your niece will send you a valentine?" he asked.

"She's too young."

"Well, do you think your sister will send you one for her?"

"No," she said quietly, "I don't think so."

"If they're not going to send you valentines," he explained, "I don't see why you should send them valentines."

"I want to, Wade," she replied. "I just want to. It's fun sending valentines. It's fun watching people's faces when they open them."

She went off by herself to find her valentines. It took her longer to pick out five than it took Wade to pick out thirteen. But then, of course, it didn't matter which ones Wade picked. Except for Ellie Nakamura's, he was only sending them to himself.

3

Betrayal

Dink left K Mart first. Five minutes later, Wade took off, carrying a large plastic shopping bag packed full of valentines.

He'd reached the corner of Third Street and City Avenue when he saw Junior and Honch speeding toward him on their skateboards. Quickly he turned, looking for a doorway or alley into which he could duck, but it was too late. They had seen him. They passed him shouting his name, screeched to a halt, picked up their boards, and walked back to him.

"Hey, man, get your board," Junior said. "We'll wait for you."

"You been shopping?" Honch asked. "What'd you get?"

"Oh, just some stuff for Auntie Mae." With both arms, he clutched the bag to his chest. "I'll just take these things home and get my board. I'll be right back." He started to run before it occurred to either of them to come with him.

He skateboarded for a while, but he couldn't concentrate. He knew two hundred valentines were waiting in the eight books lying on his bed. It would take hours to punch them all out. "Look, guys," he said, "I gotta go."

"What for?" Honch asked. "It isn't even dark yet."

"You know Uncle," Wade said. "He has fits if I'm not in by the time he gets home. Tonight he's coming back early." It wasn't much of an excuse, but it was the best he could think of at the moment.

It worked. "Yeah," Honch said. "We know Uncle. We'll see you tomorrow."

In the apartment, Wade sat on his bed and started punching, piling the scraps in the plastic bag. He punched and punched and punched until the bed was covered with valentines, and he had to move to the floor.

After dinner, he started signing them. He used the six different typefaces on his computer, plus all the handwritings he could create.

Guess Who?

Your Secret Admirer
Your Friend
An Unknown Well-Wisher
Your Valentine
Won't You Be Mine

It didn't take long to run out of anonymous phrases like that. He started using names.

Patrick Ewing
Michael Jordan
Bo Jackson
Andre Dawson
Mike Tyson

He'd read a lot of books about sports, histories, and biographies. He was able to come up with the names of stars from long ago.

Jackie Robinson
Mohammed Ali
Willie Mays
Joe Louis
Hank Aaron

Satchel Paige
Arthur Ashe

But black people weren't only sports stars. With elaborate curlicues and fancy capitals he signed other kinds of names.

Aretha Franklin
Prince
Eddie Murphy
Bill Cosby
George Washington Carver
Jesse Jackson
Oprah Winfrey
Mahalia Jackson
Nelson Mandela
Martin Luther King
Malcolm X

Maybe it was a mistake to use only black names. Maybe he'd better use some white ones too.

Ronald Reagan
Nancy Reagan

George Bush
Barbara Bush

That really got him going.

John Kennedy
Robert Kennedy
Franklin Delano Roosevelt
Dwight D. Eisenhower
Marcus Garvey
George Washington
Martha Washington
Roy Wilkins
Abraham Lincoln

Of course, like the old sports stars, a lot of these historical guys were dead. He didn't think that really mattered. No one was actually going to read the signatures on his cards. And if they did, they would figure that those names were disguises, just like "Guess Who?" and "Your Secret Admirer."

After a while, his brain went blank. He'd emptied it of every name it had ever held. He walked into the living room to get the phone book from the drawer in the telephone table.

"What are you Looking Up?" Uncle asked.

"I forgot Ali's telephone number." Wade beat a hasty retreat to his room, carrying the book with him. He opened it, and copied out names he liked the look of.

Charles Retajczyk
Eugenia Flagtown
Samuel Brescakin
Malatesta Mazzocchinni
Gerald R. Zydallis
Donatello Xerfuhs
Irwin Chocolate

and so on and so on and so on.

After he'd signed all two hundred and thirteen valentines, he had to write his own name on the envelope. That was another huge job, because it would have to be done in different typefaces and handwritings too. And he still had homework to do. It was only February 10. He had four more days. He'd get to the addresses another night.

He dumped the scraps into the big garbage pail in the kitchen, pressing them down so there was enough room. He found another bag under the sink and took it into his room. He piled all the valentines into the garbage bag and the shopping bag and stashed them under his bed. Then he finished up his homework and went to sleep.

In the van the next morning, Dink said, "There's only one problem, Wade. How're you going to stuff two hundred and thirteen valentines into that box without anyone seeing you?"

"Jeez," he admitted, "I hadn't thought about that. You got any ideas?"

She nodded. "We'll each do like twenty-five a day. The slot's pretty big. We'll probably be able to shove in ten at a time while the other kids are out in the hall getting their coats from their lockers. Mr. Peretti always goes out in the hall with them. We'll just kind of lag behind. He won't even notice, probably."

That night Wade put fifty valentines in fifty envelopes and sealed them. On one of them he wrote ELLIE NAKAMURA. On the others he wrote WADE THOMPSON, or sometimes just WADE, or COOL MAN THOMPSON, in all the different handwritings and all the different typefaces he had at his command. He put twenty-five valentines in one food-storage bag and twenty-five in another. He put one bag in his knapsack; the other he gave to Dink.

In the course of the day, he must have glanced at the valentine box a hundred times. Someone always seemed to be up there dropping valentines through the slot, but never more than one or two at a time.

The dismissal bell rang at 2:45. Mr. Peretti went out into the hall. All the teachers were required to stand in the hall while the kids got their coats out of their lockers.

Dink opened her desk and rummaged around inside as if she were looking for a misplaced homework assignment. Wade sat leaning over the math workbook as if he were so engrossed in one of the problems he hadn't even heard the bell ring. As soon as the room was empty, Wade rushed up and shoved in his bag of valentines. "Your turn, Dink," he whispered, and then stepped out into the hall.

Allison Keller and Ellie Nakamura shared a locker. "Hey, Allison," Ellie said, "I need that Garfield book I lent you."

"Marcus," Allison yelled. "You got that Garfield book I lent you? It's really Ellie's."

"No," said Ellie, "it's really my sister's, and she said I'm a dead duck if she doesn't get it back today."

"It's in my desk," Marcus said. "I'll go get it."

Marcus headed for the classroom. Ellie and Allison

went with him. Behind them trailed Wade. He hoped Dink was through dumping the valentines. He followed Allison through the door, just to make sure.

But Dink wasn't through. She was dropping the valentines in one at a time, examining each envelope before she did so, as if she had no idea what it said. A whole pile of them were still in her hand. "Heavens, Darlene," Allison said, "you're sure sending a lot of valentines, aren't you? You only had to send one, you know."

"I want to send more." Dink shoved all those she was still holding in her hand through the slot.

"I don't see why, since you're only going to get one."

Ellie stared at Allison. "How do you know that?" she asked.

"Well, maybe two. Maybe Wade'll send her one. But I don't think so." Allison turned back to Dink. "I think you like him a lot better than he likes you. Isn't that true, Dinka-dinka-dink?"

Dink couldn't answer. She'd pressed her lips tight together to keep from crying.

"How do you know I'm not sending Dink a valentine?" Marcus asked. "And I bet you anything, Angie DiCarlo is sending her one."

Ellie lifted her chin. "Maybe even *I* am sending Dink a valentine."

"You don't count," Allison said. "Wade counts. But Wade isn't sending her a valentine. Are you, Wade? Are you?"

Wade walked over to his desk and lifted the top, as if he, too, had come back into the room for something he'd left behind.

"Well, Wade," Marcus asked, "are you?"

Wade pulled a comic book out of his desk and shoved it in his knapsack. "Come on, Dink," he said. "The van is waiting."

"You see?" Allison smirked. "I told you he wasn't sending her a valentine. I told you."

Wade walked briskly out of the room. He did not run. Dink did, though. She passed Wade in the hall like a silver streak and was seated in the back of the van before he even got there. Usually he sat in the back, and Dink sat in the middle. He thought maybe today he'd sit with her, but she didn't even glance at him when he climbed into the van. So he sat in the middle and listened to the motor humming. Chatterbox Dink didn't say a word. Her lips were still pressed tight together.

Halfway home, Wade turned and glanced at Dink.

He opened his mouth as if he were going to say something. Then he realized he had nothing to say—not now. It was back in the classroom that he should have spoken. But he hadn't. He hadn't said or done a single thing. Marcus had given him the opening. All he had to do was answer Marcus's question with a yes. All he had to say was, "I'm sending Dink a valentine." It didn't matter if it was true or not. All he had to do was say it. But he hadn't.

What had happened to him? he wondered. Had he turned into some kind of coward? At Roosevelt School anyone who'd called him yellow would have ended up with a bloody nose. He'd have decked anyone who mocked a friend of his. But what had he done at Kennedy School? He'd left Dink hanging on the line to dry. And Dink was his friend. Maybe he wasn't her friend, but she didn't care about that. She was his friend anyway.

Red Hearts
and Fat Cupids

When the van pulled up to the curb in Wood-lawn Park where it always dropped them off, Wade turned to Dink. "So long," he said.

"So long," she managed to reply.

He hopped out and ran into his building. He was so disgusted with himself, he didn't want to hang out with the guys. Junior knew him too well. Junior might be able to see right through his skin to the yellow streak that ran straight from his brain to his heart.

In his bedroom, he sat for a long time staring at the blank envelopes. At last he picked up his pen. In all the different handwritings he'd created, he wrote on fifty of the envelopes

Dink
Darlene

> *Darlene Worth*
> *Dink Worth*
> *That Cute Darlene*
> *Adorable Dink*
> *My Friend Dink*
> *Darling Darlene*

and so on and so on and so on.

Next morning in the van, Dink asked for her pile of valentines. She was not one to bear a grudge. She had forgiven his traitorous behavior already. "No," he said, "I'll mail them all. You take too long. I don't want the same thing to happen today as happened yesterday."

"Neither do I," Dink said. "Don't worry, I can shove them in real fast if I have to. And I'll make sure Allison is a thousand miles away before I go near that box."

"It's all right, Dink. Just forget about it." Wade felt horrible turning her down, but he had no choice. In a couple of days she'd understand, and everything would be all right.

Dink blinked her eyes fast maybe a hundred times. Then she opened her math book and asked Wade about a problem.

Wade hung back at lunchtime to shove his fifty

valentines into the box. He didn't even notice Marcus getting paper out of the supply cabinets until Marcus spoke to him. "Hey, Wade."

He started and turned.

But Marcus didn't seem to think Wade was doing anything odd. "How many valentines you sending, Wade?"

"I sort of lost count," Wade said.

Marcus laughed. "You? You've got a calculator for a brain."

"No, I don't," Wade bristled. "I've got the same kind of brain as everyone else. The same kind of heart too." Then he remembered Marcus's question yesterday, and how he hadn't answered it. "I do, I really do," he added in a milder tone.

But Marcus didn't seem to know what he was talking about. "Well, Wade, are you?" Marcus had asked the previous afternoon. "Are you sending Dink a valentine?" was what he had meant. Now it seemed that the question that was burned into Wade's brain Marcus had already forgotten!

"All right, I believe you," Marcus said. "Don't get so excited. Anyway, I don't see anything wrong in having a better brain than other people, so long as it doesn't turn you into a snob."

"Like Allison," Wade said.

"Yeah, like Allison. Mostly, girls really stink."

Wade nodded vigorous agreement. "Are you sending any girls valentines?"

Marcus looked down at his sneakers as he rubbed one of his toes into the floor. "Well, yeah. You sort of have to. I mean if you've lived next door to a person your whole life, like I live next door to Ellie . . ."

"I sort of live next door to Dink," Wade admitted. "So I am sending her some valentines. I just didn't want to tell Allison. It's none of her business. Anyway, I think valentines are sort of babyish."

"Yeah, well maybe next year in fifth grade we won't have to bother with them."

"The girls like them," Wade pointed out.

"Then in fifth grade let the girls send them."

Wade laughed. "Yeah, let the girls send them." He and Marcus left the classroom and walked down to the cafeteria together. But once there, they separated.

Wade, as usual, sat down across from Dink. "Listen, Dink," he said, "tomorrow you tell Angie you can sit with her at lunch. It's okay, because I'm going to sit with Marcus."

"Hey, that's great!" Dink said. "That's really great."

It would certainly come as a surprise to Marcus. But

Wade thought it would be OK. At least he hoped it would be OK.

In his room that night, he stared at the one hundred and thirteen valentines that were left. He wanted to fool around with his computer. He wanted to watch TV. He even wanted to do his homework more than he wanted to write his own name on one hundred and thirteen envelopes.

He picked out the prettiest of the fifty-cent valentines and addressed it to Auntie Mae. He thought for a long time, and then addressed another to Uncle. After they were asleep that night, he'd put them by the coffeepot. Auntie Mae would smile when she saw hers the next morning. Uncle would faint.

Next he addressed two fifty-cent valentines to Carlos, two to Junior and one each to Big Bert, Ali, Scott, and Honch. The van picked him up early; before it came he'd run around Woodlawn Park sticking the cards in their mailboxes. If they lived to be a hundred, they'd never figure out where those valentines had come from. He'd have a million laughs listening to them try. He'd keep one around that he could say had been sent to him so they wouldn't get suspicious.

That meant only two fifty-cent valentines left. Wade addressed one to Mr. Peretti and one to his mother.

He'd ask Auntie Mae for a stamp and mail it tomorrow. It would get there after Valentine's Day, but he didn't think that mattered. He knew his mother well enough to realize she'd be surprised but pleased to get a valentine from him even if it arrived in April.

Next, he addressed two valentines to each of the kids in G&T—except Allison Keller. He didn't send her even one.

Fifty-four valentines remained. Looking at the pile, he wanted to throw up. If he never saw another red heart or fat, dumb cupid as long as he lived, it would be too soon. For a moment he thought he'd just bundle them up and throw them into the dumpster behind the building. But he couldn't waste them like that. They'd cost him too much effort and too much pain, to say nothing of too much money.

After work that afternoon, Auntie Mae had dragged herself into the house. "What's the matter, Mae Honey," Uncle had said. "You look Beat."

"Three more kids," she said. "I admitted three more kids today. That pediatric ward is so stuffed they had to roll in more beds. The grown-ups I can take. After all, they've had a life. But those kids, they really get to me."

Uncle made her a cup of coffee. After she drank

it, she seemed to feel much better. At supper she didn't talk about the kids. She talked about the wedding shower they were making for one of the nurses who was getting married.

But now Wade remembered the kids. In the kitchen closet he found a brown paper bag. He got out his psychedelic Magic Markers, drew hearts all over the bag and colored them in. He didn't make them all red. Some were green, some were blue, some were yellow, and some were purple. Then he wrote in huge black letters, LAMONT MEMORIAL MEDICAL CENTER PEDIATRIC WARD. When he was done he gazed at the bag with satisfaction. He thought it was really beautiful. He put the remaining valentines inside. Tomorrow morning he'd give the bag to Auntie Mae to take to the hospital.

5

I Have Hope

When Wade came out of his room the next morning, Auntie Mae hugged and kissed him. "Oh, Wade," she said, "I feel so bad. I didn't get *you* a valentine."

"Don't worry about it, Auntie Mae," he said. "I think I'll be getting plenty of valentines."

"Naturally. You've always been so popular."

"Yeah, sure."

Uncle gazed at him long and hard. "You're not so Popular up at Kennedy, are you?"

Wade gulped and shook his head.

"Because you're black?"

Wade didn't answer immediately. It seemed important to give Uncle the most honest reply that he could. Uncle didn't seem to mind waiting. "That's part of it," Wade said at last.

"Racism is always part of it," Uncle said.

"But some of the kids in the class are okay," Wade admitted.

Uncle put his hand on Wade's shoulder. Wade almost jumped back, so surprised was he at the touch. "Popularity doesn't matter," Uncle intoned. "A few Good Friends is what matters. If you have one or two Good Friends in the G&T class, you'll be all right."

Wade knew he had Dink, whether he wanted her or not. And maybe he had Marcus. He'd find that out soon enough.

"I also want to say Thank You for the valentine," Uncle went on. "The way you did the names on the computer—that came out Real Pretty."

"It's a good computer," Wade replied. "I'm glad you gave it to me." This time he meant what he said. He wasn't merely being polite, like at Christmas.

Auntie Mae glanced at the kitchen clock. "Where's the time gone to this morning? I've got to get out of here."

Wade had almost forgotten. "Wait just a second," he said. He ran back into his room and came out again carrying the glittering paper bag. "Take this to the hospital. It's for the kids in the pediatric ward."

Auntie Mae peeked inside. "Are there valentines in those envelopes?"

Wade nodded.

"That is so nice," Auntie Mae said. "That is the nicest thing I ever heard of. And to think it was my own wonderful boy who thought of it."

"Well," Wade said, "I got the idea from you."

Auntie Mae gave him another hug and kiss. Wade could feel the wetness of the tears on her cheek.

Mr. Peretti had said the Valentine's party would be at the end of the day. Wade knew that was a mistake. He should have scheduled the party for the beginning of the day. Afterwards, everyone would have been able to settle down to their work. As it was, they couldn't sit still one minute, so busy were they wondering how many valentines they'd get, and from whom. It wasn't only the girls who were wondering. The boys were just as restless and distracted. Mr. Peretti yelled at them at least seventeen times.

The only person in the class who was perfectly calm and relaxed was Wade. He knew exactly how many valentines he was getting. He knew who they were from. He knew he'd sent even more to other people than he'd sent to himself. He had nothing to worry about.

As the class clattered down to the cafeteria at lunchtime, Dink came up to him and whispered, "Are you
sure it's all right?"

"Is what all right?"

"Me sitting with Angie?"

"I'm sure. Go ahead."

Dink hurried off to Angie's table. Evelyn Torrance
and Sylvia Wertheimer sat there too. Fortunately Allison Keller did not. Wade watched Dink as she leaned
over and said something to Angie. Smiling, Angie
stood up halfway and gestured toward the chair that
faced her. Dink was smiling too, as she sat down.

Now Wade did have something to worry about. He
had to worry about what Marcus would say when he
found out Wade was accepting an invitation that was
five months old. He'd probably forgotten he'd ever
issued it.

There was nothing to do but to march over to Marcus's table, where Ed Meyer and Tony Oznick also
sat. That was probably OK. But so did Farley McNair.
That was probably not OK.

Wade carried the lunch Auntie Mae had prepared
in a brown paper bag. He dropped the bag on the
table in front of an empty chair. "Can I sit here?" he
asked.

"That's Chipper's seat," Farley said.

"Chipper's absent," Ed pointed out.

"He'll be back tomorrow," Farley said.

"There *are* six chairs at this table," Marcus noted.

"Chipper might not like it," Farley returned.

"Look, Farley, I asked Wade to sit here, a long time ago." So, Wade thought, Marcus did remember.

"You didn't check with me," Farley said.

"This is a public cafeteria. A person can sit wherever he wants. You don't like it, *you* find another seat."

Farley glanced at Tony. "That's right," Tony said.

"Oh, okay," Farley muttered, "go ahead, sit down."

Now Wade didn't know whether he wanted to sit there or not. But he'd burned his bridges. Besides, he wasn't going to do to Marcus what he'd done to Dink. He wasn't going to leave Marcus hanging on the line to dry. So he sat down. "Don't mind the crumb," Marcus said. "You get kind of used to him after a while."

Farley grunted. Wade opened his bag, took out his sandwich, and munched away steadily. With his mouth full, he didn't have to do much talking. It was all right. They talked about the same stuff any bunch of guys would talk about.

After lunch came science and social studies. Then, at last, it was time for the valentines.

"Farley, Evelyn," Mr. Peretti said, "you can be mail carriers. Take a few valentines at a time out of the box and deliver them to the person whose name is written on them."

Twenty minutes later, Farley and Evelyn were still delivering. Mr. Peretti leaned over the box and peered inside. "Cripes," he said, "I never saw so many valentines in my life. At this rate, we'll be here until five o'clock. Ellie, Tony, you'd better come up here and help."

The pile on Allison's desk was pretty high. So were the piles on Marcus's desk and Ellie's desk and many other desks. But they were nothing compared with the pile on Wade's desk and the pile on Dink's desk. Dink arranged hers neatly, one on top of the other. Occasionally, her hand reached out to flatten down the pile, but otherwise she just sat there staring at it with wide, delighted eyes.

"Well, Dink," Angie said when all the valentines were at last delivered, "aren't you going to open them?"

"Open them?" Dink sounded as if the idea had never occurred to her. "Oh, I guess so." She slit one envelope and looked at the card. She did the same with another, and another, and another. It took her a long time because she read every word on every valentine over and over before she went on to the next one. She especially read the signatures—Mike Tyson, Martin Luther King, Irwin Chocolate. She knew exactly where those valentines had come from. She looked so happy Wade thought she might just float away.

"How many valentines did you get, Dink?" Ellie asked her.

"Fifty-one," she replied.

"I only got twenty-seven," Ellie said. "And Allison only got thirty-two. So I think you got the most in the class."

"Well," Dink admitted, "I imagine a lot of them were from the same person."

"Of course," Allison said. "Your boyfriend." She shot Wade a significant glance. "Who do you think that is?"

Dink raised her eyebrows. "I haven't the slightest idea," she replied coolly. "It's all so mysterious. That's what makes it fun."

Ellie giggled. "Oh, Dink, you're a riot."

"Wade got a whole mess of valentines too," Ed said. "Who are yours from, Wade?"

There was one from Dink, of course, one from Marcus, and a few from other kids in the class. To his surprise, there was even one from Allison Keller. Maybe she sent valentines to every kid in the class. But that didn't seem like Allison. She must have picked his name, and turned green at the sight of it.

Wade pushed the real valentines aside. He picked up one of his own and stared intently at the signature, as if he'd never seen it before. "Ronald Reagan," he announced. Then he picked up another. "Bill Cosby." And another, and another, and another. "Eugenia Flagtown. Michael Jackson. Oprah Winfrey."

The class was laughing. Each time he read a name they laughed some more—except for Allison. "Who really sent you those valentines?" she called above the din.

Suddenly the whole room was silent. Every pair of eyes was fixed on Wade. "Maybe the same person who sent all those valentines to Dink," he replied.

"And who would that be?" Allison snapped.

"Oh, Allison," Wade returned, "why don't you just try guessing?"

Allison opened her mouth to fling back a retort, but Mr. Peretti got there first. "Who cares who sent them?" he said. "We know it was someone with a good

imagination. We got a good laugh out of them. Isn't that enough? Go ahead, Wade, read the rest."

Allison shut her mouth. Wade read the other signatures. Then Mr. Peretti brought out the refreshments. Mrs. Nakamura and Mrs. Meyer, the class mothers, had baked heart-shaped cookies colored with red food coloring and sprinkled with sugar. Mr. Peretti had bought soda and paper napkins and paper cups decorated with hearts. "Marcus, Wade, Angie, would you please help me serve?" he asked. Marcus poured the soda, and Wade carried the cups around to the desks. Angie passed the cookies.

When everyone else had their food, Mr. Peretti and Wade stood side by side, their cups outstretched for Marcus to fill with soda. "Well, Wade, what do you think of G&T now?" Mr. Peretti asked. "Is it so bad? Are you going to come back next year?"

"I don't know," Wade said. "I have to see how Easter and Memorial Day work out."

"Well, at least you're smiling," Mr. Peretti replied. "I have hope."